D1263769

To: Our families and friends

"Let's do our best and the best will follow"

First published in Great Britain in 2015 by Brainchild Publications Ltd, Wisteria Camrose House, 2a Camrose Avenue, London, HA8 6EG.

www.thefallofsnow.com
www.brainchildpublications.com
Email: hello@brainchildpublications.com

ISBN 978-0-9932475-0-7

A CIP catalogue record for this book is available from the British Library

Printed in the United Kingdom

THE FALL OF SNOW™

Written by
Mark Ampaw & George Roberts

Illustrated by
Jeremy Salmon

brain Child
PUBLICATIONS

Early one morning, a little boy called Asare climbed out of his bed, looked through the window and cried out, "Wow!" He saw the ground covered in something that looked like white cotton wool. Asare had never seen anything like it before.

All of a sudden, Asare saw cotton wool flying across the sky. Then he noticed that his friends Ziko and Kai were throwing the fluffy stuff at each other.

Asare ran down the stairs to meet his friends, but as he reached the door, Grandpa stopped him and said, "Take your sister Aya with you." He told Asare and Aya that the cotton wool was actually called snow, and he said that they should wear warm clothes because it was freezing outside.

Asare and Aya met with Ziko and Kai and began to throw snow balls at each other. After playing for awhile, Ziko said, "let's build a bunch of snow people".

Together, the children built four snow people – two snowmen and two snow women.

Aya worked on the bodies, Ziko made the heads,
Asare worked on the legs and Kai made the arms.

After the children had finished making the snow people, Grandpa called them to come into the house for lunch.

When they had finished eating, the children left the house and ran to see the snow people – only to find they were gone. They began to search high and low.

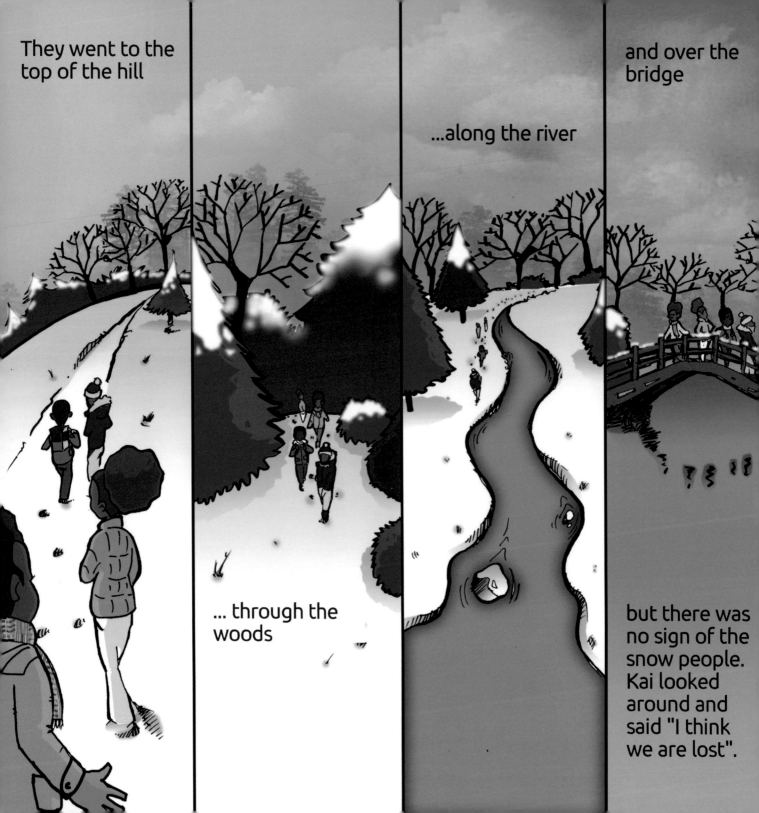

They went to the top of the hill

... through the woods

...along the river

and over the bridge

but there was no sign of the snow people. Kai looked around and said "I think we are lost".

Suddenly, Asare felt a cold, icy hand on his shoulder. "Are you looking for us?" said one of the snow women in a frosty voice. The children looked around and saw they were surrounded by the snow people. They began to scream "Ahhhhhh!" Then one of the snowmen said in a loud, deep voice, "Now you will work for us, because you are all so creative."

The snow people made the children build a snow castle and a snow kingdom, complete with a snow army.

The children also had to build an ice dome over the kingdom to block out the sun...

.....a rocket ship out of snow, so they could fly above the clouds.

Beneath the snow kingdom, they built a snow tunnel to allow the snow people to travel underground. The children also overheard the snow people talking about changing all humans into snow people.

"Did you hear that?" said Asare to the others. "Yes! What are we going to do?" Kai replied. "We need to find a way out of here before they change us into snow people!" said Ziko. The children started looking around for a way out. "I think we're trapped," said Aya.

"Look! there's a hole in the dome," said Kai, pointing towards it. "But nobody is small enough to fit through that hole," Ziko replied.

"I am," Aya answered. Asare said to Aya, "Go and get help!" So Aya headed for the hole.

A few snow soldiers saw what was happening and tried to stop Aya, so Asare, Ziko and Kai threw snowballs at the soldiers to stop them catching the little girl as she escaped.

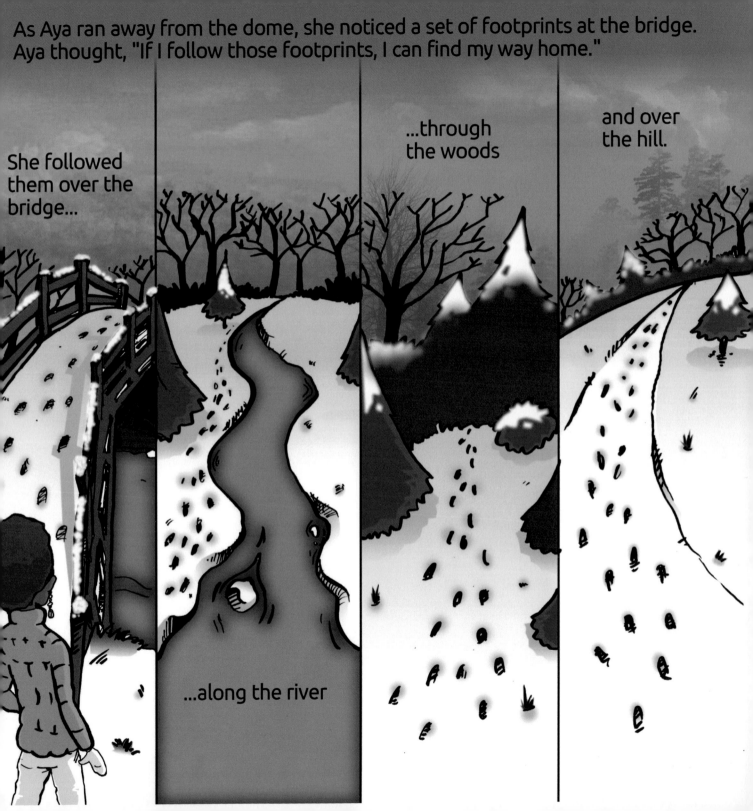

Aya finally arrived at Grandpa's house and told him everything that had happened. Grandpa said in a soft voice, "Calm down. When the first flower sprouts, everything will be OK." Then he whispered a few words to her before saying loudly, "Now go back and tell the others." Aya headed back to the snow kingdom to tell the other children what Grandpa had said.

As Aya entered the snow kingdom, she saw that Ziko, Kai and Asare were chained up. The snow people approached and said together, "Now the time has come to turn you all into snow people."

Aya shouted out, "Wait! Look at the flower!" Everyone turned and looked at it.

Moments later, the children noticed that the ice dome was melting. The kingdom, the rocket ship, the army, the children's chains and, finally, even the snow people began to melt, too.

Aya then told the children the message Grandpa had given her. "Grandpa said we should always be thankful for the beautiful sun!!!"

"The Four Seasons"

GET YOUR TICKETS FOR...

A NIGHT AT THE CIRCUS

For tickets and more visit:
www.brainchildpublications.com